# Disney · PIXAR

## ANNUAL 2008

**Editor: Jaine Keskeys**
**Art Editor: Phil Williams**

EGMONT
We bring stories to life

First published in Great Britain in 2007
by Egmont UK Limited
239 Kensington High Street, London W8 6SA
© Disney Enterprises, Inc./Pixar

ISBN 978 1 4052 3177 0
1 3 5 7 9 10 8 6 4 2
Printed in Italy

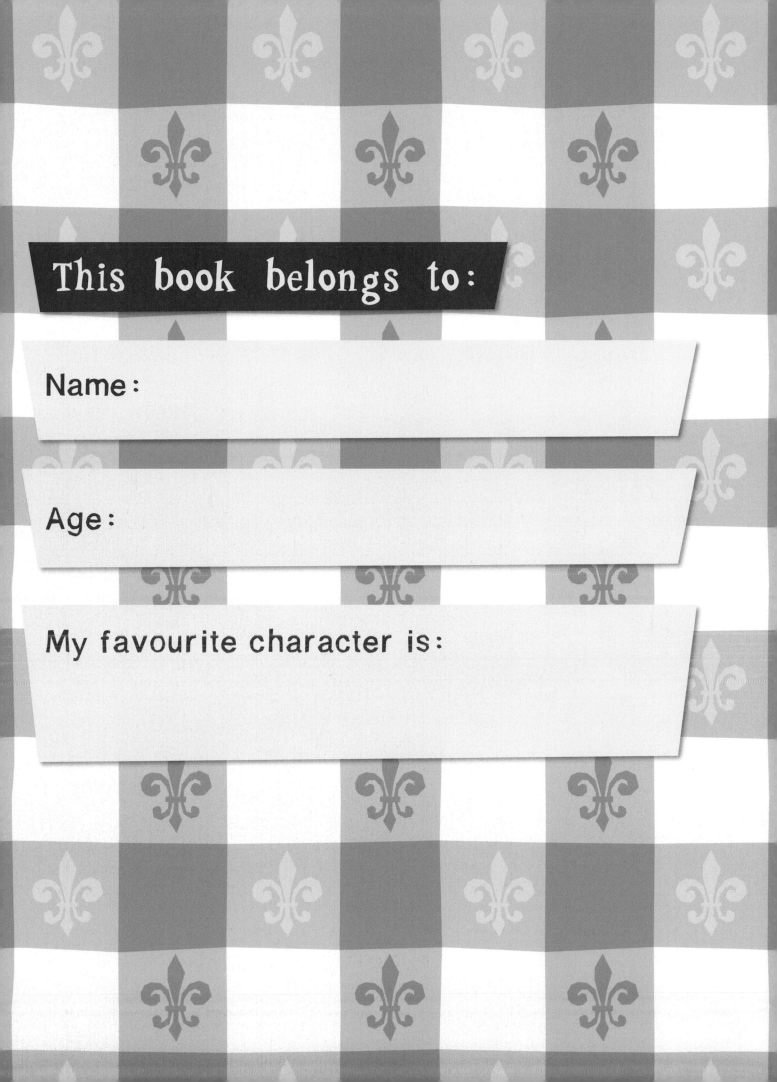

# This book belongs to:

Name:

Age:

My favourite character is:

# Disney · PIXAR

## ANNUAL 2008

# Kitchen capers

**1.** Remy, the rat, dreamt of becoming a chef. One day, in the kitchen of his favourite restaurant, he saw Linguini, the garbage boy, fixing a spilt soup.

**2.** Linguini was adding one wrong ingredient after another. "I have to do something," thought Remy. So, he ran down to help the shocked Linguini!

**3.** With amazing speed, Remy tossed some carefully chosen ingredients into the soup. He knew exactly which ingredients would taste good!

**4.** Just in time, the soup was ready. A waiter took a bowlful out to a customer in the restaurant. Suddenly, Remy and Linguini heard shouting.

**5.** Skinner, the restaurant's mean chef, was coming! He would be very angry if he saw a rat in his kitchen. Linguini quickly hid Remy under a colander.

**6.** "How dare you cook in my kitchen!" Skinner shouted. He was very angry with Linguini, but he couldn't sack him because the soup tasted delicious!

**7.** While they were talking, Remy made a run for the window. But Skinner spotted him. "Catch it and dispose of it!" Skinner shouted to Linguini.

**8.** But instead of getting rid of Remy, Linguini made a deal with him. "I'll let you out of the jar, if you promise to help me cook," said Linguini.

**9.** Remy agreed. So, Linguini hid Remy in his shirt and they returned to the kitchen. That night, Linguini and Remy went home to practise cooking.

**10.** Remy showed Linguini how to cook by tugging his hair from inside his hat. With Linguini's help, Remy's dream had come true – he was a chef!

The end

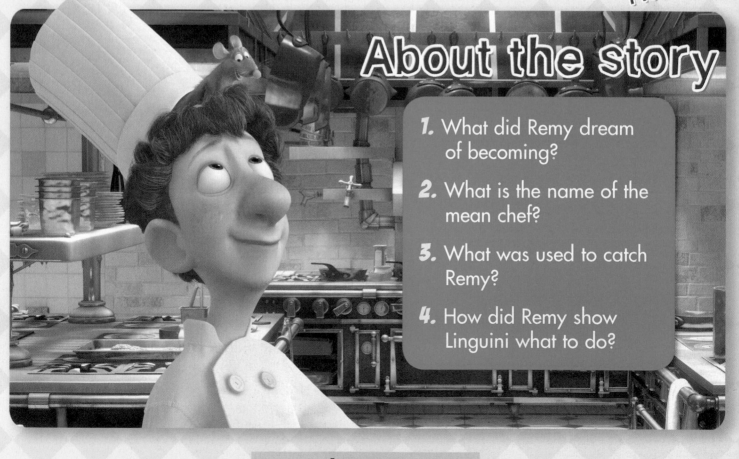

# About the story

**1.** What did Remy dream of becoming?

**2.** What is the name of the mean chef?

**3.** What was used to catch Remy?

**4.** How did Remy show Linguini what to do?

**Answers:**
1. A chef. 2. Skinner. 3. A jar. 4. By tugging on his hair from inside his hat.

# Core colours

Finish the dot-to-dot to find out what Emile is about to eat and then add some yummy colours!

# Cooking changes

Remy is making some delicious soup. Before he's finished can you find five differences in the bottom picture?

**Answers:**

1. Remy's arm has moved. 2. An onion has appeared. 3. There are extra herbs. 4. The pan handle has disappeared. 5. A spoon is missing.

# Right route

Remy has always dreamt of being a chef. Which route should he take through the maze to reach the kitchen?

**Answer:** Route c.

13

# Rat race

Play this game with a friend. Who will reach the cheese first?

**You will need:** a die and two counters.

**1** START

**2**

**3**

**4**

**5** Stop to eat bread! Go back 2 spaces.

**6**

**7**

**8** Trip over sor strawberrie Miss a turn

# How to play

Place the counters at START. Take it in turns to throw the die and then move along the path the same number of spaces as the number thrown. If you land on an instruction, follow what it says. Whoever reaches the cheese first, wins!

**19** Find a carrot! Move forward 2 spaces.

**20**

**18**

**17**

**21**

**25** FINISH

**16** Roll on an onion! Move forward 1 space.

**22** Stop to eat an apple! Miss a turn.

**23**

**24**

**15**

**10**

**11** Lose your way! Go back to START.

**12**

**14**

**9**

**13**

# Chef shades

Help Linguini to become a better cook by adding a dash of colour!

16

# Shadow search

Remy's hiding in the shadows. Draw a line to link each matching pair. Which shadow doesn't have a match?

a

b

c

d

e

f

g

# Fluffy friend

Emile is Remy's brother. Remy's here to show you how to make your own fluffy Emile. He can live in your bedroom!

**You will need:** a ball of brown wool, card, a pencil, scissors, a cup, colouring pencils and sticky tape.

**1** Draw around the top of the cup on to the card. Draw another circle inside the first circle, using the smaller end of the cup. Do this twice.

**2** Cut out the circles and place them together. Then, wind the wool around and around the two pieces of card until the centre hole has disappeared.

**3** Ask a grown-up to help you cut through the wool, between the two pieces of card.

Note to parents: adult supervision is recommended when sharp-pointed items, such as scissors, are in use.

**4** Loop a length of wool between the two pieces of card and tie tightly. The end of this will be Emile's tail! Remove the card.

**5** Finally, cut out Emile's face and stick it on to card. Tape it on to the pom-pom!

©Disney/Pixar 2007

**19**

# Countdown

Remy is teaching Linguini how to cook. How many of each object can you count in the panel below?

🫕 = ☐   🥄 = ☐

👨‍🍳 = ☐

**Answers:** Pans – 6, spoons – 5, hats – 4.

# Remy's recipe

Add some spicy colours to this picture and complete Remy's recipe.

# Tuning trouble

**1.** Every morning, Radiator Springs woke up to the sound of Sarge and Fillmore's music battle. They both thought their music was the best!

**2.** "My military marches get everyone up and ready for the day," insisted Sarge. "My grooves send happy vibes to the whole town," replied Fillmore.

**3.** The residents of Radiator Springs were fed up with the battle, so Doc decided to settle things. He called Sarge and Fillmore into his courtroom.

**4.** "You can both still play your music," said Doc. Sarge and Fillmore were puzzled. "But take turns! Play your music on different days," ruled Doc.

**5.** So, on Monday morning, Sarge's marching music filled the air. He loved listening to his tunes without the extra sounds of guitars and flutes.

**6.** Then, on Tuesday morning, Fillmore was delighted to play his soothing sounds. There were no trumpets or drums thumping in the background.

**7.** But the other cars in the town soon found that Sarge and Fillmore's music sounded terrible on their own. They asked Doc to change his mind.

**8.** The next day, everyone was glad to hear the music battle start up again. "I guess some things are best left as they are!" sighed Doc.

# Radiator race

**Luigi's Casa Della Tires**

QUALITY · SERVICE

Luigi's CASA DELLA TIRES

Follow in Lightning McQueen's tracks and speed around the shops in Radiator Springs! Can your friends keep up?

## Before you play
● You will need counters and a die. This game can be played with up to four friends. Find a colourful counter for each player and see how quickly you can make it back to McQueen!

## How to play
● Each player must place their counter on one of the four shops.
● Take it in turns to throw the die and move the counters around the course in a clockwise direction. You must pass every shop and then get back to your own shop.
● Next, you must move along your coloured path, to the centre. Lightning McQueen is waiting for you there!

TOW MATER

**Tow Mater Towing and Salvage**

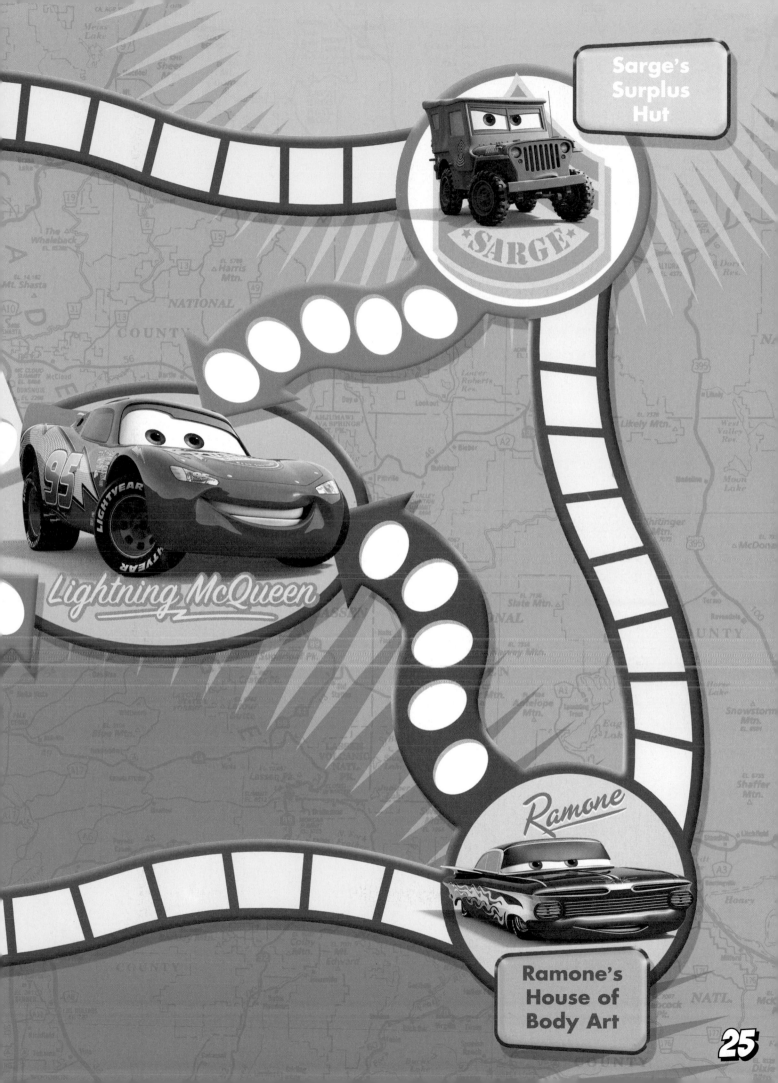

Sarge's Surplus Hut

Lightning McQueen

Ramone

Ramone's House of Body Art

25

# Shade Sally

Sally is a speedy sports car! Quickly colour her in, using the small picture to guide you.

26

# Picture puzzle

Finish the bottom picture of McQueen! Trace over the grey lines to complete the picture, then add colour.

27

# Racing rosette

This big rosette is fun to make and will look great on your bedroom wall! You can give one to your friends, too, when they win a race!

**You will need:** white card, crêpe paper, scissors and glue.

**1** Cut out a circle of white card. Stick blue crêpe paper on to the back of the card circle, scrunching it as you go.

**2** Do the same with white crêpe paper and then red crêpe paper. Use a bigger piece of crêpe paper each time, so that it sticks out.

**3** Cut out a strip of red crêpe paper and a strip of blue crêpe paper. Cut a V-shape in one end of each strip. Stick the strips behind the card circle.

Note to parents: adult supervision is recommended when sharp-pointed items, such as scissors, are in use.

**95**

Write your racing number in the centre of your rosette to show that you are the winner!

# Rocky road

Lightning McQueen is racing down this rocky road to Radiator Springs. Lead the way and answer the questions as you go!

**Start** →

**3** Which two cars have a music battle?

**4** What colour is Sally the sports car?

30

1 Who works in the House of Body Art?

2 Who has a Surplus Hut?

5 What number is written on McQueen's side?

→ **Finish**

Welcome to
ESTABLISHED 1909
**RADIATOR SPRINGS**

**Answers:** 1. Ramone. 2. Sarge. 3. Sarge and Fillmore. 4. Blue. 5. 95.

31

# Car questions

**1** Which of the following would you NOT get during a pit-stop?

**a** more fuel
**b** new tyres
**c** a cup of tea
**d** a windscreen clean

**2** Can you work out which Radiator Springs residents are in the shields below?

a
b
c
d
e

**3** Can you spot three things that are wrong with the second image of Sally?

# Cool colours

**Doc was once a famous race champion! He's a cool car so give him some cool colours, using the small picture as a guide.**

33

# Turtle time

Marlin and Dory have joined the East Australian Current and found some new friends. There's fun to be found, too!

**1** How many in the group are swimming upside-down?

**2** Add a pattern to this turtle's shell!

**3** Are there more big or more small turtles?

**4** What do the numbers on Crush's shell add up to?

1 3 2 1

N e m o 5

Look at the letters in the bubbles. Who is Marlin thinking about?

**6** Point to the turtle with its eyes shut!

**Answers:** 1. Two. 3. Big turtles. 4. Seven. 5. Nemo. 6. Top right turtle.

35

# Mates maze

## Whose path, between the bubbles, leads to Nemo?

Tad

Sheldo

Squirt

Pearl

36

**Answer:** Pearl's path.

# Pebble pals

**Make some sea-creature friends for your room, with these colourful painted pebbles!**

**You will need:** pebbles, poster paint, glue, paintbrushes and googly eyes.

Paint colourful fish on to some smooth pebbles and then stick on googly eyes.

# A bad breakfast

**1.** One morning, Marlin and Nemo went to the Drop-off for breakfast. They gasped in wonder, as tasty pieces of cake drifted down around them.

**2.** "It's raining food!" giggled Nemo, as he went to take a bite. "Wait!" cried Marlin. He'd noticed that each piece of cake was attached to a fishing line.

**3.** "As if there weren't enough bad things in the sea, like barracudas and jellyfish! Now we've got to put up with humans, too!" groaned Marlin.

**4.** "When the fish wake up, they'll bite the food before they realise! We've got to keep them away!" cried Marlin. He quickly warned two other fish.

**5.** As more and more fish arrived at the Drop-off, it became harder and harder to warn them all. "We can't get to everyone in time!" puffed Nemo.

**6.** Suddenly, Marlin had a great idea. "I know! We need to play them at their own game!" he thought. So, Marlin swam out to sea, to find a buoy.

**7.** Marlin knew that's where lots of seagulls would be. "MINE!" screeched the seagulls, as Marlin surfaced. They chased him back to the Drop-off.

**8.** When the seagulls saw the cake on the boats, they forgot about Marlin. The fish cheered, as the fishermen got fed up with the seagulls and roared away!

# Floating fun

The Tank Gang are making their escape! Finish the drawing and then colour them in.

40

# Class changes

Mr Ray is taking his class on a school trip. Can you spot 10 differences in the bottom picture?

# Pairing up

School has finished and everyone needs pairing up with a parent!

**You will need:** a coloured pen for each player.

# How to play

Players take it in turns to draw a line linking a matching pair of fish. You cannot cross a line that has already been drawn, or touch the seaweed or other fish. The player who links the most pairs is the winner.

# Tricky triple

Join the Incredibles as they tackle three tough teasers.

**1** Violet's strongest force field adds up to 10. Which one is it?

**a** 3 1
2 2

**b** 2 3
3 1

**c** 1 4
2 3

**d** 1 2
2 4

**e** 3 1
1 2

**2** Which colour hole is Elastigirl stretching into?

**3** How many bricks are missing from the hole that Mr. Incredible has made?

44

**Answers:** 1. c. 2. Green. 3. 15.

# Family fun

**Dash and Bob always make an Incredible mess around the house when they're having fun, until they have a Super idea!**

One Saturday, Bob and Dash were playing a game of heroes and villains in the front room.

"I am the evil Baron Von Ruthless and nothing can escape me!" cackled Bob, as he tried to catch Dash.

"No one can trap a Super kid like me!" laughed Dash. He dodged Bob, sprinted around the walls and dived behind the sofa.

Dash grabbed the cushions and pelted Bob with them. Bob laughed and lifted the sofa above his head.

Suddenly, there was a loud crash. The sofa had hit the lampshade and cracked it!

Dash turned quickly and ran straight into Helen, who was carrying a basket of laundry. The basket flew out of her hands and the laundry landed on the floor.

Helen groaned. "Why can't you two have normal family fun, like throwing a ball or playing with trains?" she sighed.

"Because they're ultra-boring," muttered Dash.

Bob knew it was unfair to wreck the house every time they played. "OK, we'll go to the park and have some normal family fun," he said.

At the park, they threw a ball back and forth, like all of the other fathers and sons. Within five minutes, Bob and Dash were both fed up.

"Can't you give me a throw that's a bit harder to catch?" whispered Dash.

So, when no one was looking, Bob threw the ball as hard as he could.

The ball flew so fast that no one could see it. Dash cheered and bolted after it.

When Bob finally caught up, Dash was standing by some locked gates, without the ball.

"The ball landed somewhere in there. I think we've lost it," cried Dash.

"That's the railway yard where I do all my training," said Bob.

"Cool!" cried Dash, as Bob grabbed him and jumped over the gates in a single leap. There were trains everywhere.

"OK, I'll race you. Whoever finds the ball gets a double scoop of ice cream on the way home!" challenged Bob.

So, Dash whizzed around the railway yard and Bob lifted trains, searching for the ball. They were having a great time.

"So, did you manage to have some normal family fun?" asked Helen, later.

"Sure! We played with a ball and messed around with trains, like you suggested!" giggled Bob.

The end

47

# Who's who?

**Can you work out which character each of the questions is about?**

Elastigirl

Violet

Frozone

Jack-Jack

E

Dash

**1** Who is sitting?

**2** Who makes Super suits?

**3** Who is stretching?

**4** Who is chilly?

**5** Who is running?

**6** Who is disappearing?

**Answers:** 1. Jack-Jack. 2. E. 3. Elastigirl. 4. Frozone. 5. Dash. 6. Violet.

# Cool cups

**You will need:** two polystyrene or paper cups, red paint, a paintbrush, scissors, glue, a pencil and string.

Cut out the Incredibles logos on the right. Paint the cups red and then stick a logo on to each one.

**2** Make a small hole in the bottom of each cup. Cut a long length of string and thread it through both cups, tying a knot in each end.

**3** Hold one cup and ask a friend to hold the other. Stand far apart, so that the string is tight. Now, talk into your cup while your friend holds their cup to their ear...

WILL YOU TALK IN AN INCREDIBLE CODE?

Note to parents: adult supervision is recommended when sharp-pointed items, such as scissors, are in use.

# Memory match-up

Have you got an Incredible memory? You'll need one to win this game

You will need: 18 squares of card, one to cover each picture.

# How to play

Take a good look at the pictures, before covering them all with pieces of card. Take it in turns to lift two cards at a time. If the pictures underneath match, the player keeps the cards and has another go. If the pictures underneath do not match, the player replaces the cards and the next player has a go. The player with the most cards at the end is the winner!

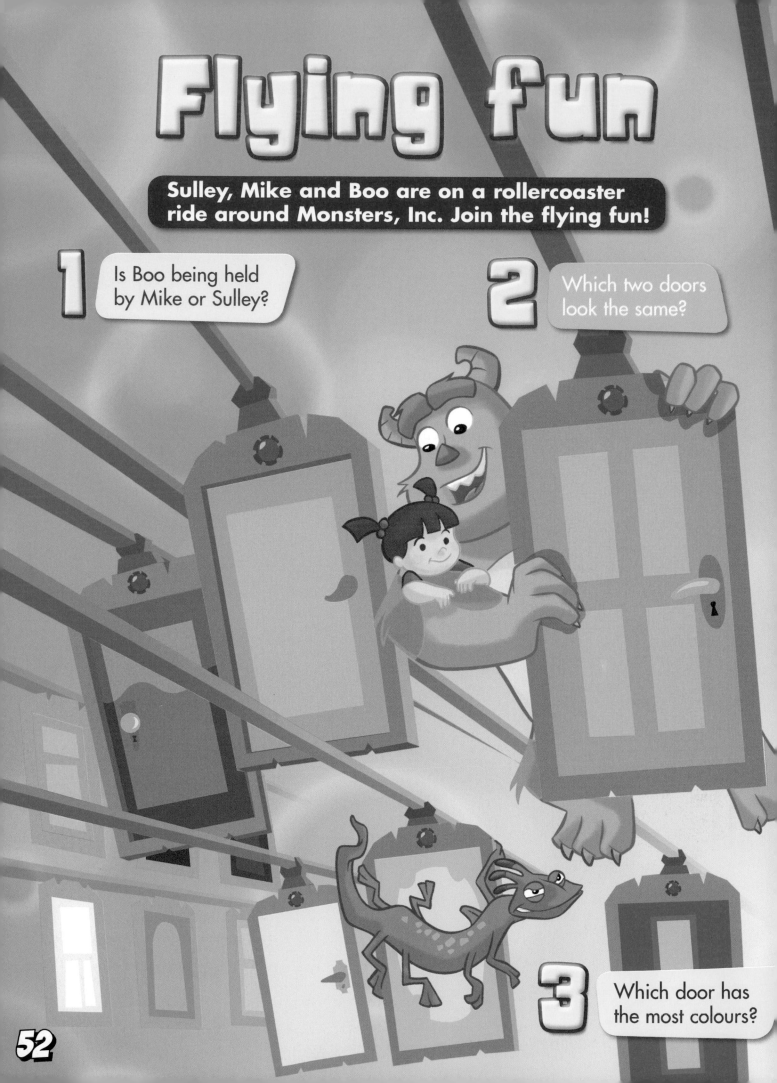

**4** Which monster is following Sulley, Mike and Boo?

**5** Where is a key?

**6** How many door handles can you count?

# Monster mysteries

Sulley is having trouble with these tricky teasers. Help him to find the answers!

**1** Can you put the scream canisters below in the right order, to find out who filled them?

**2** Who can you see through the keyholes? Match each one with the correct name.

Celia    Mike    Waternoose

R  N  A  A  L
L      D

a        b        c

**3** Which colour door has the highest total and the loudest scream behind it?

2
3
1
1

3
1
2
3

1
4
3
2

2
1
2
3

**54**

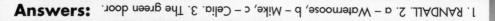

# Reveal Randall

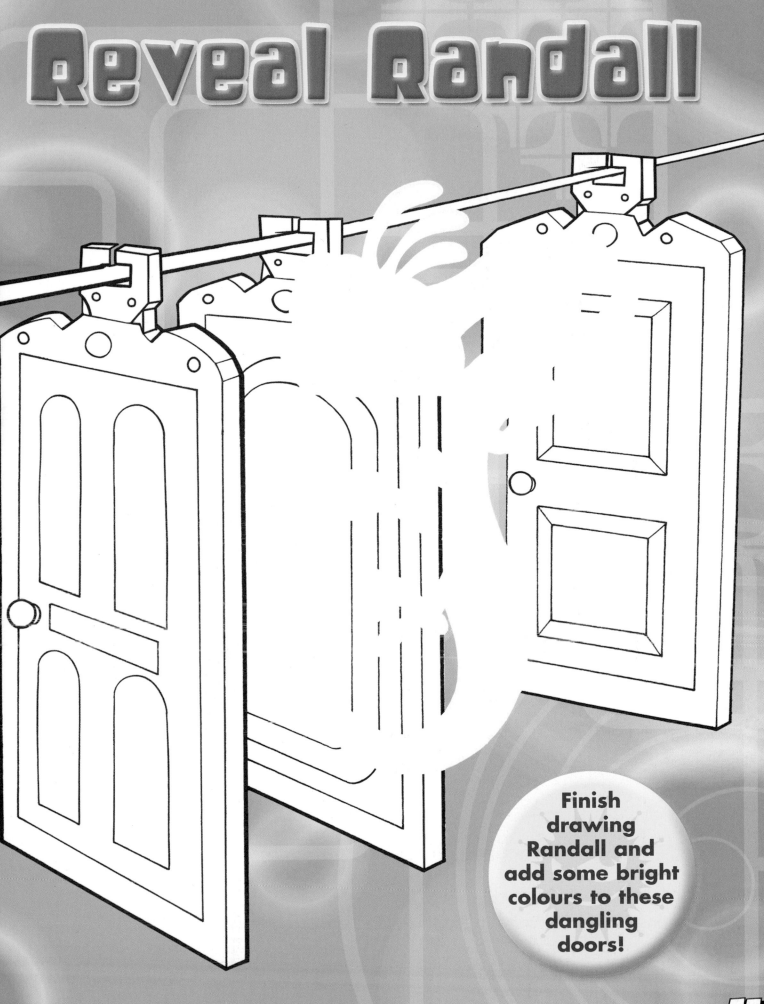

Finish drawing Randall and add some bright colours to these dangling doors!

# Sulley's roar

**1.** One sunny day, Sulley and Mike were on their way to work. "Let's see if I can make the highest scare total, ever!" said Sulley.

**2.** "No problem! Any kid who hears your roar will fill two scare canisters!" chuckled Mike. Just then, Sulley noticed a sad monster mum in her garden.

**3.** "What's wrong?" asked Sulley. "My little monster's school uniform is still wet. By the time it's dry enough to wear, he'll be late!" she groaned.

**4.** "Stand back!" said Sulley. He took a deep breath and roared at the uniform. The blast dried it in seconds. "Thanks!" cheered the happy mum.

**5.** A little further along the road, Sulley and Mike met some builders. They were having trouble knocking down a wall. "Stand back!" Sulley told them.

**6.** He let out another enormous roar. The force was so strong that the wall crumbled into a thousand little pieces! "What a guy!" clapped the workers.

**7.** When Sulley and Mike finally got to work, all the roaring had made Sulley's throat sore. "Without your roar, you can't scare!" panicked Mike.

**8.** As Sulley went through the first door of the day, Mike was sure they'd have a low scare total. "We'll be lucky to fill one canister," he sighed.

**9.** But Sulley had an idea. His throat was too sore to do the jump and growl so, when the child opened his eyes, Sulley whispered, "Roar!" instead.

**10.** The surprised child screamed so loudly that it filled three canisters! "Even with a tiny roar, you're still the best Scarer in the business!" cheered Mike.

The end

# About the story

1. How did Sulley dry the little monster's uniform?

2. Who did Sulley help next?

3. What happened to Sulley's throat?

4. How many scare canisters did the child fill?

**Answers:**
1. He roared at it. 2. Some builders. 3. It became sore. 4. Three.

# Odd one out

All the monsters in Monstropolis look pretty odd but can you spot one in each line that is different from the others?

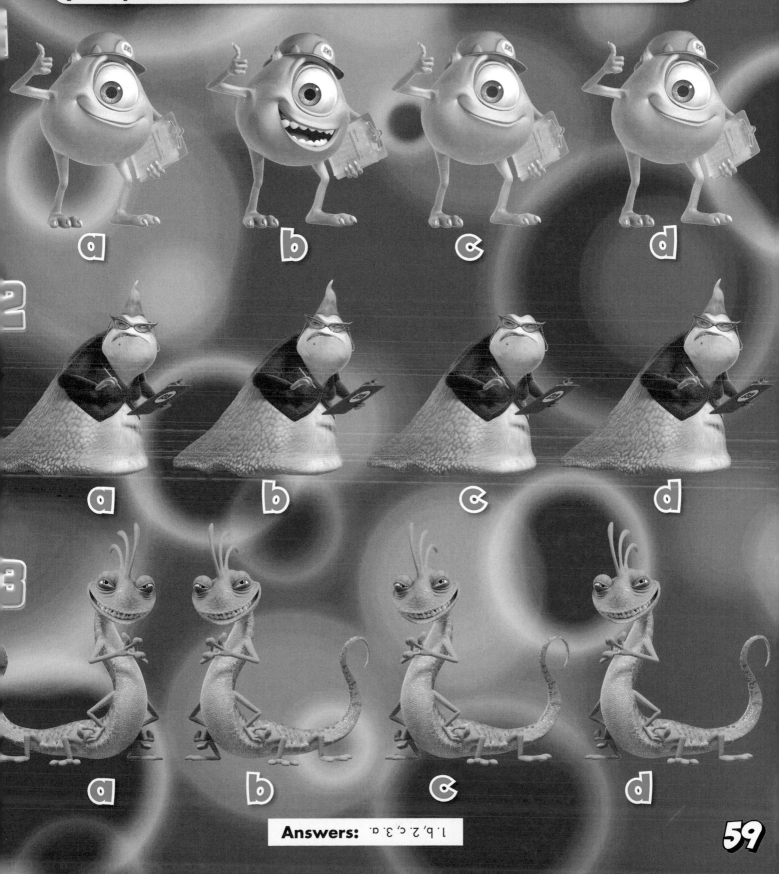

# Toy teaser

Rearrange each pile of blocks to spell a number from one to five. Which toy has which number?

**Woody**

**Buzz**

**Jessie**

**Bullseye**

**Rex**

# Cowboy colours

This cowboy likes to make an entrance! Finish the drawing and give Woody some colour.

# Bedroom boogie

Join in the fun and answer these questions, as the toys boogie around Andy's bedroom!

**1** How many musical notes can you count?

**2** What colour is Jessie's hat?

**3** What name is written on Buzz's shoe?

62

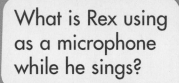

**4** What is Rex using as a microphone while he sings?

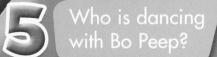

**5** Who is dancing with Bo Peep?

**Answers:** 1. Three. 2. Red. 3. ANDY. 4. His tail. 5. Woody.

63

# Making music

Andy has found an old keyboard but it's too shy to play. Join Woody and the gang, as they teach it how to have fun again!

One afternoon, Andy ran into his bedroom, holding a big, dusty box. He put the box on to the floor and pulled out an old keyboard.

"Let's see if this thing still works!" said Andy. He sat down and started to push buttons and press switches.

Nothing happened, though. "Oh, rats!" said Andy, looking upset.

"Poor Andy!" thought Woody, as he watched his owner walk away. "He really wanted to play with that toy. I wonder what's wrong with it?"

When Andy had gone, Woody called Buzz over, to try to find out what was wrong with the keyboard.

"This thing has more buttons than my spaceship!" said Buzz, staring at the rows of switches. "I wonder which one turns it on?"

"Andy tried them all," said Woody. "I think it's broken."

"No, I'm not!" cried a funny electrical voice. Woody and Buzz jumped in surprise. The keyboard was working, after all!

"Well, howdy, Mr Keyboard!" said Woody. "Why didn't you play for Andy, earlier on?"

"I was too scared," whispered the keyboard, looking sad. "I've been sitting in a box for so long that I've forgotten how to have fun."

"That's really awful!" cried Buzz. "Having fun is what toys do best!"

"Come on then, everybody!" shouted Woody. "Let's show this keyboard how to have a good time!"

All of the toys gathered round. Soon, everyone was singing and dancing and enjoying themselves.

"Wow! This is great!" said the keyboard. He started to play, adding merry music to their singing.

"Hey!" laughed Woody. "You really rock!"

Soon, the keyboard was playing so loudly that Andy heard him from downstairs and came running up, to see what was happening.

As quick as a flash, the toys stopped dancing and fell to the floor. The only one who was still making merry music when Andy burst in, was the keyboard!

"Hooray!" cried Andy. "It does work, after all!" So, he sat down and played with the happy keyboard, until it was time for bed.

The end

# Party time

Brighten up this toy party by giving Jessie, Woody and Bullseye a lick of colour!

66

# The line-up

The toys are all marching across the room.
Can you work out who is where in the line?

**1** Who is at the front?

**2** Who is in the middle?

**3** Who is two places behind Rex, the dinosaur?

**4** Who is in front of Woody?

**Answers:** 1. Hamm, the pig. 2. Rex, the dinosaur. 3. Buzz. 4. Slinky, the dog.

# Quick quiz

Did you enjoy reading your Annual? Finally, look back through the pages and answer this quick quiz!

**1** What did Remy dream of in Kitchen capers?

**2** How many shops did you visit in the Radiator race?

**3** What did the seagulls screech in A bad breakfast?

**4** On which page did you see this picture of Jack-Jack?

**5** What colour door is Mike holding on to in Flying fun?

**6** Who is at the back of the line in The line-up?

68

**Answers:** 1. Becoming a chef. 2. Four. 3. MINE! 4. Page 48. 5. Purple. 6. Jessie.